I CAN READ ABOUT

DOGS
AND
PUPPIES

Written by J. I. Anderson

Illustrated by Judith Fringuello

Troll Associates

A dog will share your happy times.
He likes to be your friend.
You can even tell him secret things
no one else knows.

Dogs like to play. But did you know
they can do other things too?

A dog can learn to obey commands,
and help with many jobs.

He can protect sheep and cattle,

guard the house at night,

and help hunt wild birds.

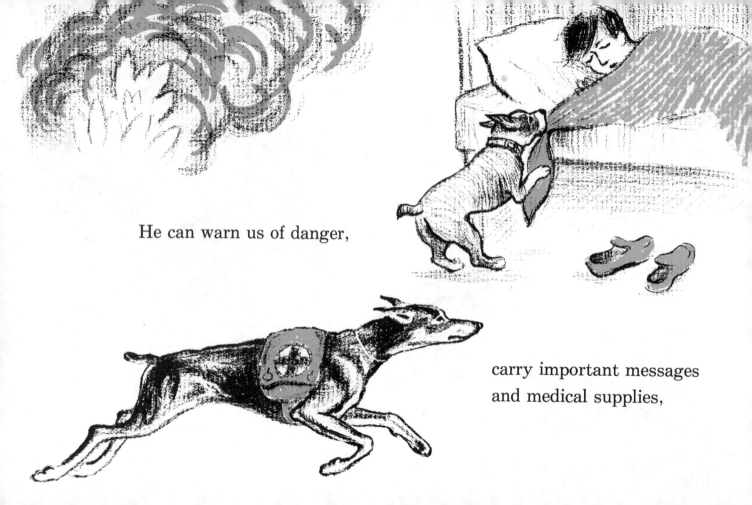

He can warn us of danger,

carry important messages
and medical supplies,

and find missing people.

He can be a "Seeing Eye"
for blind people.

In the cold northern countries,
teams of dogs pull carts
and sleds over the
frozen snow and ice.

A dog is a helpful companion, as well as
a friendly playmate.

The dog has served man faithfully for thousands of years.

A cousin of the wild wolf, he was tamed by primitive man a long time ago, in the Stone Age.

Man soon discovered that the dog could help him hunt other animals, by following their scent.

Man shared his cave and warm fire with his new friend,
who protected the cave from wild animals.

FOX

WOLF

Many kinds of animals belong to the dog family. Some are tame, others are wild. They are all called **canines**.

COYOTE

JACKAL

The fox, the wolf, the coyote, and the jackal are untamed, or wild dogs.
They live mostly on meat and hunt smaller animals by their sight or scent.

The different kinds of tame dogs are called breeds.
There are thousands of mixed breeds in the world,
and more than 350 pure breeds.

When a dog's parents are the same breed
—for instance, when both are beagles—
he is called a purebred dog. He can receive
a certificate called a pedigree and
win prizes at dog shows. Purebred dogs
are divided into several groups.

There are SPORTING DOGS

The cocker spaniel is one of the most popular sporting breeds.
At one time, he was trained to hunt wild birds, especially the woodcock.
That's why he is called a **cocker**. "Spaniel" means he originally came from Spain.

The shiny red coat of the Irish setter makes him a handsome sight to see.
He is a cousin of the spaniel and loves to go hunting. He was taught
to crouch or "set" when he found a wild bird. Then the hunter would toss a net
over both the dog and bird, and catch the bird!

There are HOUNDS

The playful little beagle loves to chase rabbits.
With his keen sense of smell, he can find them almost anywhere—
and he can run just as fast! The beagle is small enough for any home
and is a lively pet for boys and girls.

Bouncing along on his short little legs, the dachshund makes
us laugh. But his funny hot-dog shape had a very special purpose.
Long ago, he helped farmers catch pesty badgers, by wiggling down the holes
to their underground homes. In fact, **dachshund** in German means
"badger dog."

There are WORKING DOGS

Handsome and intelligent, the brave collie has won many medals
for saving lives. He is also a friend and helper of the shepherd.
A collie will guard a herd of sheep all day and night,
in all kinds of weather.

The German shepherd is an
eager worker, usually devoted
to only one master.
As a guard dog,
he earns respect
for his loyalty.

This intelligent dog often becomes a
"Seeing Eye" dog. He leads his blind master safely through
busy streets, never forgetting that his master's life depends on his alertness.

There are TERRIERS

The word **terrier** means "of the earth." The Scottish terrier is famous
for chasing mice. And "Scotty" usually catches them, too!
He has a black, stiff-haired coat and long chin whiskers.

The wire-haired fox terrier
used to be a hunting dog
famous as a fox chaser.
He was very brave and would
quickly dig into the ground
to surprise foxes in their tunnels.
Today they are popular family pets
and favorite show dogs.
Because they are lively and smart,
they learn tricks easily.

There are NONSPORTING DOGS

The perky poodle is famous for performing circus tricks. Watch him dance or walk a tightrope or even flip a somersault! His unusual haircut was used many years ago to help him get wild birds from ponds and lakes.

His hair was shaved off most of his body so he could swim more easily. But some was left on his chest and legs to protect him from the cold water.

The Dalmatian loves to travel alongside a horse.
In the days when fire engines were pulled by horses,
he was a busy member of many fire departments.
Today, the Dalmatian often rides on fire trucks
as the firemen's mascot!

There are TOY DOGS

Toy dogs are very small, and usually stay indoors most of the time. The Pekingese (pee-keh-NEEZ) lived in the palaces of ancient China, two thousand years ago. The emperors put these little dogs in the sleeves of their robes to keep their hands warm. Although he is small, the Pekingese has great courage, and his barking scares away much larger animals.

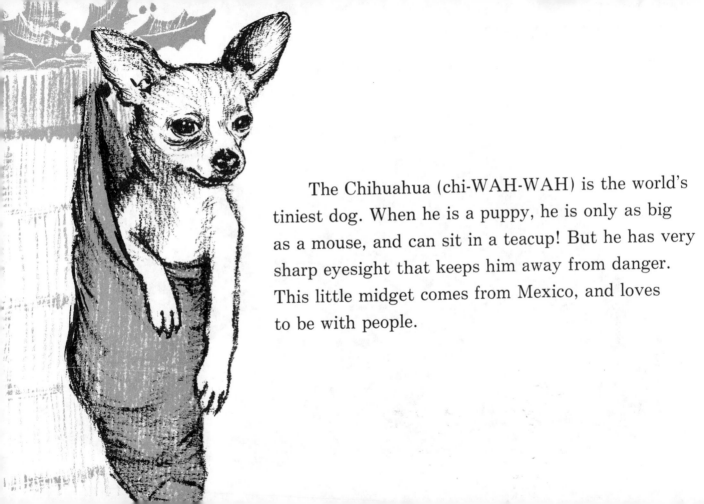

The Chihuahua (chi-WAH-WAH) is the world's tiniest dog. When he is a puppy, he is only as big as a mouse, and can sit in a teacup! But he has very sharp eyesight that keeps him away from danger. This little midget comes from Mexico, and loves to be with people.

WHICH PUPPY FOR YOU?

There are so many kinds of dogs, it is hard to choose one for a pet. Sometimes it is easier to choose if you know how big a puppy will grow, and what he will look like when he is grown.

A mixed breed puppy is just as good a pet as a purebred—maybe even better! There are more kinds of mixed breed dogs in the world than any other kind. They come in all sizes, shapes, and colors. How he looks when he grows up may be a big surprise. How he behaves depends partly on how you treat him.

It really doesn't matter
what kind of puppy you choose.

Most puppies are friendly and lovable—
especially when they are your very own!
Just be sure to choose one
that is healthy and happy.
He should be about 8 weeks old,
and have bright, clear eyes and a shiny coat.

Like all babies, a puppy needs
plenty of love and attention, and
plenty of sleep. Make him a bed out of a soft, old blanket,
and put it in a warm place in the house. At first, he may cry a little
when left alone, but soon he will get used to his new home.

A puppy should be fed several times a day, in small amounts. Give him milk and meat mixed with cereal, such as canned dog food. As he gets older, you can add dog biscuits, dry meal, and most kinds of meat. Keep fresh water in a spill-proof dish where your puppy can always reach it.

Here is a Feeding Chart for your puppy:

8 weeks to 3 months old:	4 meals each day
3 months to 6 months old:	3 meals each day
6 months to 1 year old:	2 meals each day
Adult dog:	1 meal each day

Puppies need to be protected from sickness and infections, just like people. A veterinarian will tell you what vitamins and medicines your puppy should take to grow up strong and healthy.

Do not wash your puppy until he is 6 months old. He might catch cold when he is wet. As he gets older, wash him only once in a while— maybe once a month—so his skin does not get dry.

Brushing is good for your dog. It makes his coat
smooth and shiny, and helps keep him from scratching.
You'll be proud of how nice he looks,
and he will feel better!

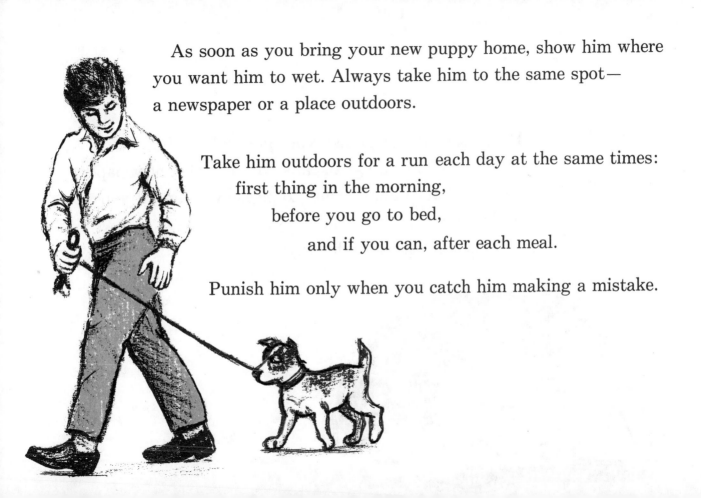

As soon as you bring your new puppy home, show him where you want him to wet. Always take him to the same spot—
a newspaper or a place outdoors.

Take him outdoors for a run each day at the same times:
first thing in the morning,
before you go to bed,
and if you can, after each meal.

Punish him only when you catch him making a mistake.

Be gentle. Do not punish your puppy harshly.
Just a scolding, or a light spank with a folded newspaper
is enough. Your puppy wants to please you, and if you
train him the same way each day,
he will soon learn the right way.

Teach your puppy good manners. Try short lessons, repeated several times each day. Teach him to come when he is called, to sit, to lie down, to "heel" or walk close to your side, and to get used to walking on a leash. When he does these things, reward him with a gentle pat, and a lot of praise.

Repeat each command several times.
You will have to be very patient because
puppies would much rather play.
Teach him only one thing at a time.
If you want to know more about training and
caring for your puppy, the library or
pet shop will be happy to help you.

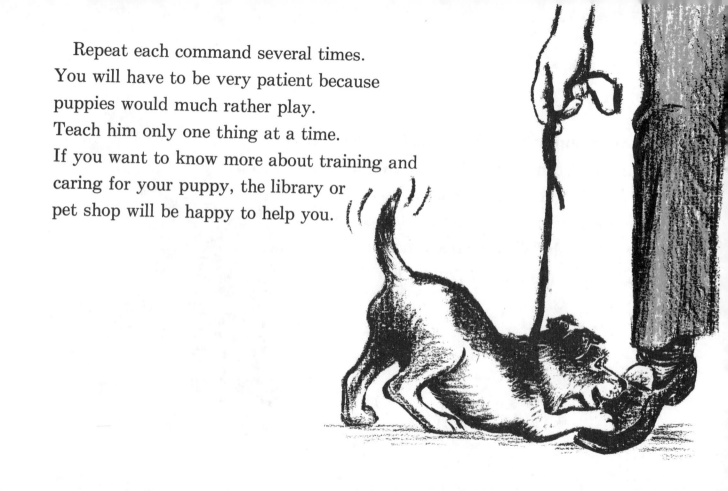

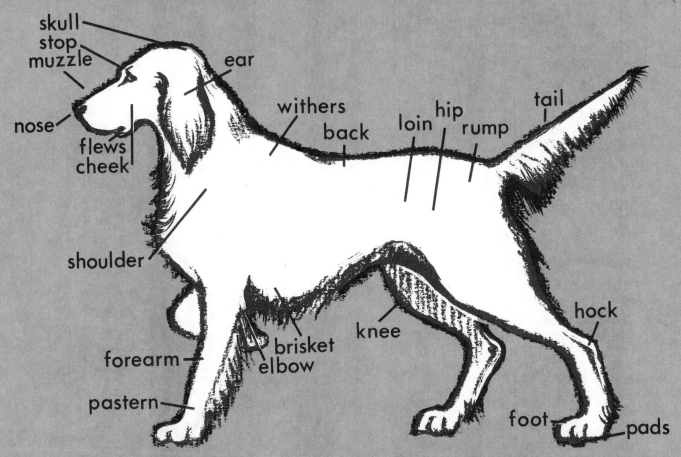

skull
stop
muzzle
ear
nose
flews
cheek
withers
back
loin
hip
rump
tail
shoulder
knee
hock
forearm
brisket
elbow
foot
pastern
pads

These are the different parts of a dog. You may want to study them later.

FUN FACTS ABOUT DOGS

Did you know that
there is one dog that cannot bark?
He is the basenji (ba-SEN-jee),
an African hound.

When he stands up on his hind legs,
the Irish wolfhound is taller than an average man.

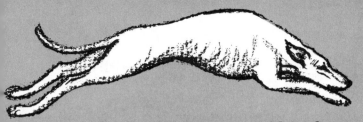

The fastest dog in the world is the greyhound. He can run 40 miles an hour (64 kph).

The oldest known breed is the saluki (sa-LOO-kee). His picture appears on the walls of ancient Egyptian tombs.

The Chow, a dog from China, has a blue-black tongue.

The mastiff was used by
the ancient Greeks
to hunt lions.

The world's first space traveler
was a Russian dog named Laika.
She was sent into space
in a satellite in 1957.

Did you know that a 2-year-old dog is equal in age to a man 24 years old?

All puppies are born blind.
Their eyes open when
they are about 12 days old.

One of the heaviest dogs in the world is
the Saint Bernard. He can weigh as much as
180 pounds (81 kg).

Long ago, dogs worked very hard, and did many difficult jobs. But today, most dogs are pets. Most love people, and are happiest when they belong to someone special, like you!

A dog will share your happy times,
and cheer you up when you are sad.

He will play with you for hours,
or sit quietly at your feet.

He will listen to all your secrets,
and never tell anyone.

He is your friend.